Patricia Kite *Down in the Sea:*

THE OCTOPUS

ALBERT WHITMAN & COMPANY • Morton Grove, Illinois

To Rachel and Israel Evenchick,
who were very brave, and came to America

Thanks to Dustin Chivers, Senior Curatorial Assistant,
Department of Invertebrate Zoology,
California Academy of Sciences,
San Francisco, for his help.

Library of Congress
Cataloging-in-Publication Data
Kite, L. Patricia. 1940–
Down in the sea: The octopus / L. Patricia Kite.
p.   cm.
Summary: Describes the physical characteristics
of the octopus, where it lives, and how it
moves, eats, mates, and protects itself.
ISBN 0-8075-1715-1
1. Octopus—Juvenile literature. [1. Octopus.]
I. Title. II. Title: Octopus.
QL430.3.02K57 1993   92-12284
594'.56—dc20   CIP   AC

Cover and interior design:
Karen A. Yops.

The text typeface is Optima.

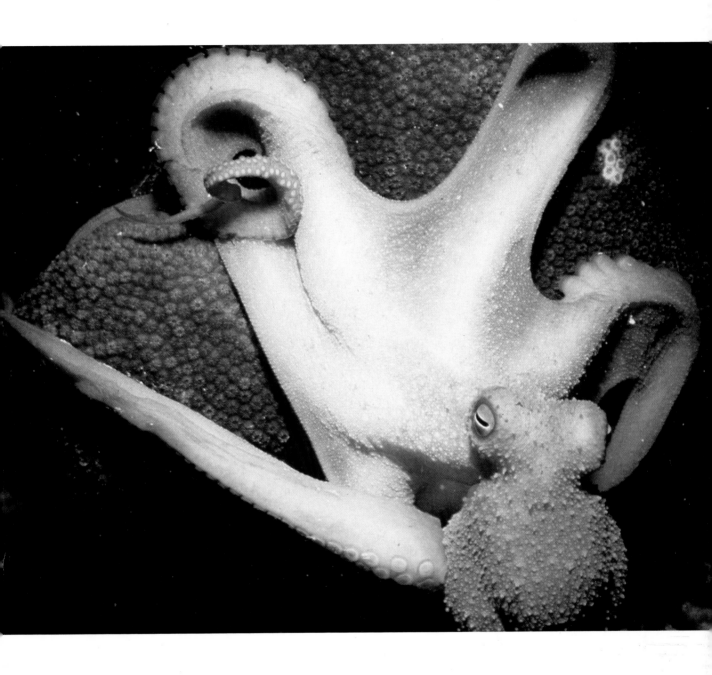

Monster octopi.
Oh, my!

Some are bigger than a merry-go-round.
Many are smaller than your hand.

But all are so shy
that sometimes a diver
only sees eyes.

Octopus (one)
octopi (many)
like to hide.
They are so soft—
not a single bone!
Even big ones can squeeze
into very small places
like holes in sunken ships,
rock caves, jars, and pots.

Some people think the whole baglike top
of an octopus is its head.
But most of this is stomach and other body parts.
Only the tip-top, around the eyes, is the head.

Octopi eat lobsters, crabs, clams,
fish, and sea snails. Yum!
When food is near,
out sneaks a long arm.
Each arm has many sucker discs
that look like white rubber cups.
Big octopi can have two thousand discs—
little octopi, just a few.
Sucker discs are nose, tongue,
and strong fingers
to an octopus.

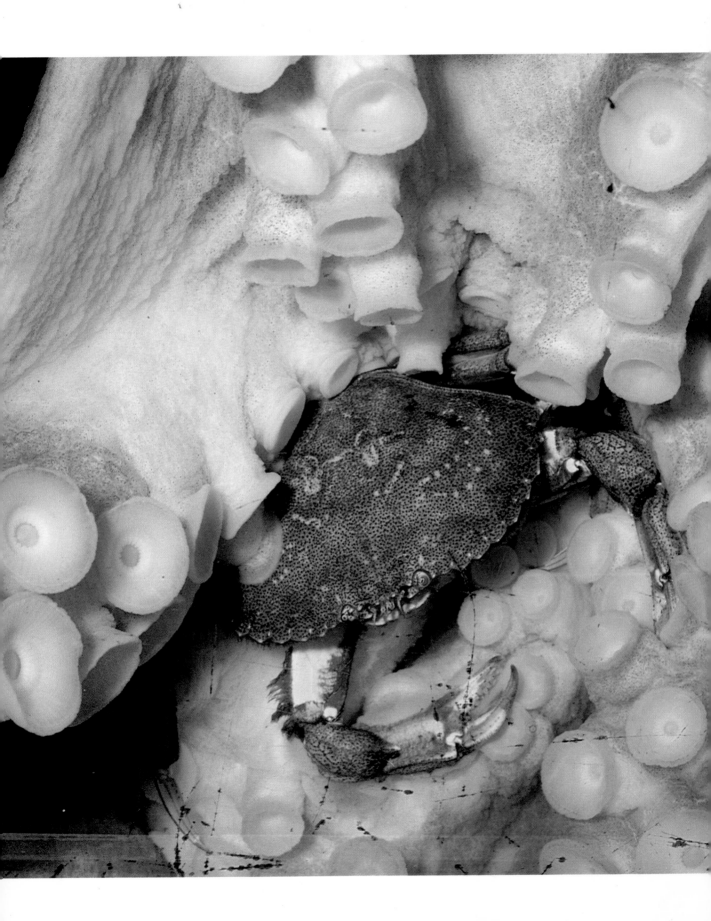

Ooops!
A sucker disc feels a crab.
Quickly, two sucker discs grab it.
Before biting the crab shell
to scrape up the tasty insides,
the octopus gives off a poison
that makes the crab stop moving.
(Dinner is no fun if it's wiggling!)

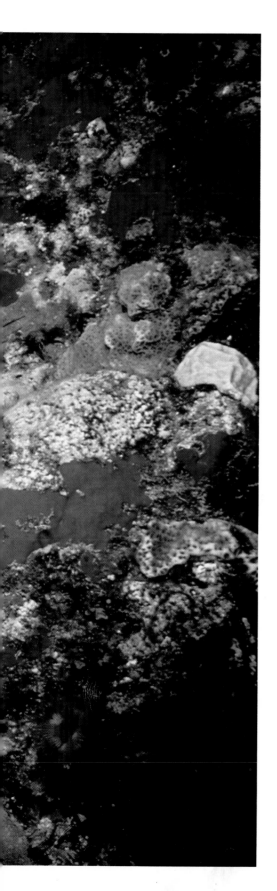

Sometimes an octopus goes out
looking for a meal.
It moves two arms, two arms,
two arms, two arms,
crawling easily along the ocean bottom.

An enemy is looking for a meal, too . . .

An octopus can swim very fast.
It sucks water into a space in its body,
then . . . whoosh!
the water shoots out through a special tube
like a jet blast.

This blast moves the octopus
frontwards, backwards, or sidewise.
Zip-zip—off it goes!

Sometimes an enemy swims fast, too.
But now there's a brown cloud!
Where is the octopus?
Octopi have a special body part
that makes dark ink.
While the enemy looks in the ink cloud,
the octopus swims home.

An octopus can change color!
If angry or scared,
it turns red, like a berry.

But once safe,
it turns tan, or green, or white
so it looks like the things around it.
It can become smooth or very bumpy.

Octopi don't live together,
but sometimes male and female
meet to mate.

After mating, the female goes home
to lay eggs in long bunches.
She hangs the eggs from the hiding-place ceiling
like rice-covered shoelaces.
One female may lay thousands of eggs.
She dusts them lightly with her suckers
and blows water over them,
never leaving, never eating.
(After the babies are born,
she will die.)

In one to three months, babies appear,
looking like octopi, but very small.
They swim out of the cave, or jar, or shipwreck.
A lot of hungry fish are waiting . . .
Few babies reach grown-up size.

Divers see big and small octopi;
octopi see big and small divers.
When not scared,
octopi can be very curious.
Out goes an octopus arm.
What's that?
A monster person!
Oh, my!

ABOUT OCTOPI

Octopi live in every ocean. There are one hundred fifty to two hundred species, with bodies ranging from little to big. But even a thumb-sized octopus can have very long arms—twenty-four inches long!

Chomp! Sometimes an enemy bites off an octopus arm. But wait a while. Some types of octopi can grow a new shorter arm to replace the missing one.

To seek food or avoid an enemy, octopi eyes keep a good watch on their surroundings. Octopi eyes can move in almost a full circle. For a better view, one eye may look one way, the other in a different direction. A few octopi have eyes that can rise up like submarine periscopes.

Escape is an octopus specialty. When danger threatens, out comes a cloud of dark ink. For a short time, this ink stays in a shape resembling an octopus. Confused, an enemy lets the real octopus scoot away. (Scientists think the camouflage ink also blocks an enemy's sense of smell, giving the octopus an even better head start.)

Soon the octopus is in a safe hiding place: rock cluster, underwater cave, or discarded jar. An octopus has no bones or shell, and only a small, hard, hidden beak. It can squeeze into some very tiny places. A ten-foot-wide octopus can squish through a four-inch hole!

Sometimes an octopus builds its own special hiding place. It collects stones, shells, and ocean garbage, piling them up to comfortable shelter size. The same home may be used year after year.

Octopi live alone. But sometimes divers see a male octopus with an arm reaching out and touching a female. This is a special arm used only for mating. It carries sperm from the male to inside the female.

Octopi are the smartest invertebrate animals (animals without backbones). If scientists place food inside a corked jar, an octopus will figure out how to remove the cork. Octopi have short-term memory, too. Repeat the experiment within twenty-four hours, and the octopus will take the cork out right away.

Octopus, octopi is easiest to say. But *octopus, octopuses* is fine, too. Just so you know!

PHOTO CREDITS   Cover: Animals Animals/ © G. I. Bernard, OSF; p. 1: Animals Animals/© Waina Cheng, OSF; pp. 2, 14: © Ed Robinson/Tom Stack & Associates; p. 3: © Herb Segars; pp. 4, 15, 23: © Dave B. Fleetham/Tom Stack & Associates; p. 5: © Kjell B. Sandved/Photo Researchers, Inc.; pp. 6–7: Animals Animals/ © Anne Wertheim; pp. 8, 13, 20: © Carl Roessler; p. 9: Animals Animals/ © Zig Leszczynski; pp. 10–11: © Carleton Ray/Photo Researchers, Inc.; pp. 12–13, 19: © Al Grotell; p. 16: © F. Stuart Westmorland/Tom Stack & Associates; pp. 17, 21, 22: © Fred Bavendam; p. 18: © F. Stuart Westmorland.